Mickey's Roundup

A LEVEL PRE-1 EARLY READER

By Susan Ring

Illustrated by Loter, Inc.

DISNEP PRESS

New York

Disney PRESS

Copyright © 2008 by Disney Enterprises, Inc. All rights reserved. Published by Disney Press, an imprint of Disney Book Group. No part of this book may be reproduced or transmitted in any form or by any means, electronic or mechanical, including photocopying, recording, or by any information storage and retrieval system, without written permission from the publisher. For information address Disney Press, 114 Fifth Avenue, New York, New York 10011-5690.

First Edition
Library of Congress Cataloging-in-Publication Data on file
ISBN 978-1-4231-1425-3

Manufactured in Malaysia
For more Disney Press fun, visit www.disneybooks.com

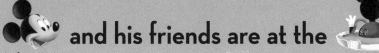 and his friends are at the .

Mickey Mouse   Clubhouse

The doorbell rings. is at the door.

Professor Von Drake

Professor Von Drake has a big  .

box

asks Mickey to watch the box.

Professor Von Drake

Professor Von Drake will be right back.

 comes to say hello.

Goofy

Look out,  ! Look out for the

Goofy

 !

box

Oh, no! 1, 2, 3, 4, 5, 6, 7, 8, 9, 10

come out of the  .

box

Numbers are everywhere!

Time for a roundup!
, , and  put on their

Minnie   Mickey   Daisy

cowboy hats.

 has a .  keeps score.

Goofy   lasso   Donald

They will count back, from 10 down to 1.

Mickey and his friends will need help.

Oh, Toodles!

Toodles has the Mouseketools.

Toodles has an  🐘 elephant , a 🧤 baseball glove ,

and a ❓ Mystery Mousketool .

uses his 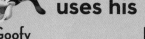.

Goofy   lasso

But 10 will not move.

Oh, Toodles! We need a

Mouseketool!

 picks the .

Mickey   elephant

An elephant is big and strong.

The 🐘 puts 10 back in the 📦.

elephant   box

 gets 9 and 8.

Minnie

Minnie puts 9 and 8 back in the .

box

Look at 7!

Goofy's  cannot make

lasso

7 stop.

Oh, Toodles! We need a Mouseketool!

 uses the to get 7.

Mickey   baseball glove

Mickey puts 7 back in the  .

box

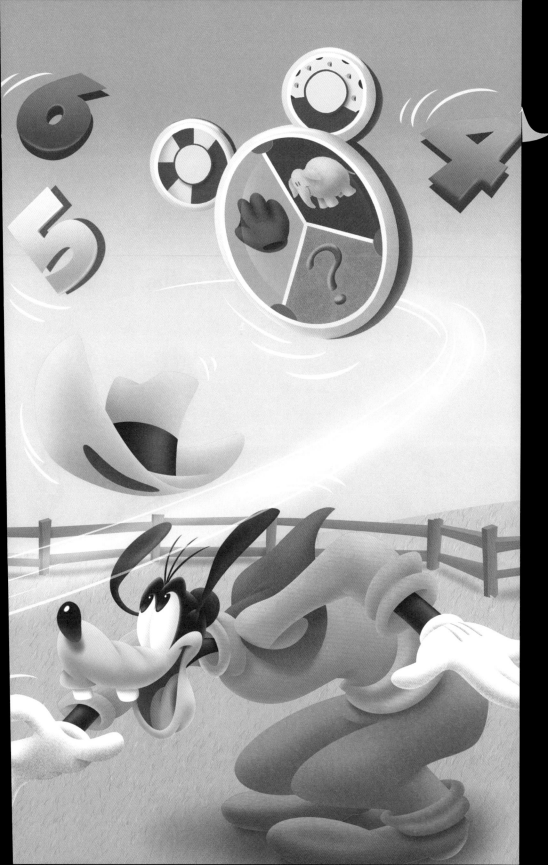

Numbers 6 and 5 buzz like little .

bees

 jumps. First she gets 5.

Daisy

Then she gets 6.

 puts 6 and 5 back in the .

Daisy   box

Where are 4, 3, and 2?

They are hiding!

4 and 3 are in the big .

2 is in the little tree.

tree

We have you now!

They must hurry. 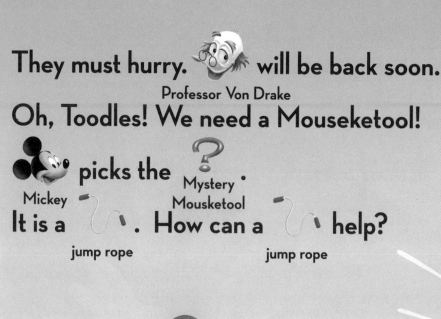 will be back soon.
Professor Von Drake

Oh, Toodles! We need a Mouseketool!

picks the ?

Mickey   Mystery
           Mousketool

It is a   . How can a   help?

jump rope   jump rope

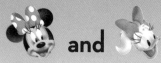 and  play jump rope with 1.

Minnie   Daisy

1 jumps right into the  .

box

Just in time!

 is back.

Professor Von Drake

Professor Von Drake thanks for

Mickey

taking good care of the  .

box

"Anytime," says Mickey.

"It was easy!"